A L I S

D0410117

Merbaby

by Penny Kendal
and Claudia Venturini

ABERDEENSHIRE
LIBRARY & INFO SERV

Kendal, Penny

Merbaby   )

JS

3001131

Evans

For my Friday workshoppers – Angela, Jo, Vivien
and Kay, with thanks - P.K.

First published 2009
Evans Brothers Limited
2A Portman Mansions
Chiltern St
London W1U 6NR

Text copyright © Penny Kendal 2009
© in the illustrations Evans Brothers Ltd 2009

All rights reserved. No part of this publication
may be reproduced, stored in a retrieval system
or transmitted in any form, or by any means,
electronic, mechanical, photocopying, recording
or otherwise, without the prior permission of
Evans Brothers Limited.

British Library Cataloguing in Publication Data

Kendal, Penny.
  Merbaby. -- (Skylarks)
  1. Children's stories.
  I. Title II. Series
  823.9'2-dc22

ISBN-13: HB 978 0 237 53907 8
ISBN-13: PB 978 0 237 53894 1

Printed in China by New Era Printing Co. Ltd

Series Editor: Louise John
Design: Robert Walster
Production: Jenny Mulvanny

Contents

Chapter One

Anna saw it first. They were standing in the rock pool staring down.

"Look, look! There's a fish!" she said.

"One of those tiddly ones?" asked Joe.

They'd found two tiny fish already and a crab, which had nipped Joe's finger. He was only four but he hadn't cried.

"No – a much bigger one," said Anna.

"I didn't see it," said Ellie. She was the oldest and had the fishing net. She swirled it round in the water.

"Can I have a turn with the net?" Anna begged.

"OK, but give it back when I ask you," said Ellie.

Anna nodded and took the net quickly. She dipped it into the water. She pulled the net up three times, but there was only seaweed and more crabs.

"Give me the net now," said Ellie.

"Just one more go," said Anna, and she plunged the net deep into the pool.

"Look!" she cried.

There it was. The fish filled the net and its tail flapped. The scales were green and shimmered like pearls.

"It's got fingers," said Joe.

"You mean fins," said Ellie.

"No, look – real hands," said Joe.

He was right. There was something strange about the fish. It had tiny pink arms, and hands with chubby fingers, just like a baby's.

The fish wriggled and flipped over. They all gasped. A face was looking up at them. It definitely wasn't a fish's face. It was a baby's face. It was pink, with two baby eyes, a baby nose and a baby mouth.

"What is it?" asked Joe. "It's weird."

"It's like half-fish and half-baby," said Anna.

Ellie spoke quietly. "I think it's a mermaid. I think it's a baby mermaid."

Chapter Two

"A merbaby," breathed Anna. She put her hands slowly into the net and gently lifted it out. It felt very strange. With one hand she held the slippery fish tail. In her other hand she held the soft pink baby head. The face looked up at her. The eyes were big and green and beautiful.

"I think she likes you," said Joe.

"Let me hold her," said Ellie.

"No – I found her," said Anna.

"How does she breathe in the water and out of it?" asked Joe.

"Look – she has gills like a fish and she must have lungs like us too," said Ellie.

"Do you think we can keep her?" asked Anna.

"We ought to look after her," said Ellie. "She must have lost her mum and been left behind here by the tide. She won't last long if no one looks after her."

"How do you look after a merbaby?" asked Anna.

None of them knew.

"We could ask Mum," said Joe.

"I don't think we should tell Mum," said Ellie. "Mum might make us put her back and I want to keep her. She'll have to be our secret."

Anna nodded. But they both looked at Joe. He was not very good at secrets.

"Joe, you do want us to keep her, don't you?" Anna said gently.

Joe nodded.

"Then don't tell Mum, OK? Do you promise?"

Joe nodded again.

"Tip the crabs out of the bucket, Joe. We can hide her in that."

Ellie took the bucket from Joe. She filled it with water from the rock pool.

"Come on, Anna, put her in."

"I want to carry the bucket," said Anna. "It was me that found her."

"She's not just yours," said Ellie.

"Quick! Mum's coming!" said Joe.

Chapter Three

"Hurry!" said Ellie.

Anna gently put the merbaby in the bucket and let go. "Don't worry," she whispered. "We'll look after you."

Ellie pulled the bucket away and put it down behind a big rock. "Remember Joe, keep your mouth shut," she warned.

Mum had reached them. "Time for lunch, I think," she said, and she took Joe's hand. "Have you found anything interesting?"

Ellie told her about the little fish and the crabs.

"Can I see?" Mum asked.

"We put them back in the water," said Ellie.

"Well done," said Mum. "I'm sure they are happier there. Where's the bucket?"

"I've got it," said Anna, picking it up. She began to walk ahead.

Back at the cottage, Anna sat beside her bed and lifted the merbaby from the bucket. The big eyes looked at her for a moment and then scrunched up. The mouth turned down and opened wide. The merbaby was crying but no sound was coming out.

Ellie came into the room. "What are you doing? Mum's calling us for lunch," she said.

"The merbaby's crying," said Anna. "I think she needs lunch, too."

"We should have kept those tiny fish for her," said Ellie.

"What's for lunch?" Anna asked.

"Egg sandwiches," said Ellie. "I can keep her a bit of mine."

Ellie was bossy but she was also silly sometimes.

"I don't think she'll eat egg sandwiches," said Anna.

"She's only a baby. Maybe she'll drink some milk," said Ellie.

"Yes," said Anna. "There's milk in the fridge. I'll get my doll's drinking bottle. We can put it in there."

Mum was calling them again. Anna had to leave the crying merbaby in the bucket. On the stairs, Joe pulled at Ellie's arm. He was making a strange noise with his mouth closed.

"What's the matter, Joe?"

He whispered. "You said I have to keep my mouth shut, but how can I eat my lunch with it shut?"

Anna and Ellie laughed. "You can open your mouth," said Ellie. "Just don't say anything about what we found, OK?"

Joe nodded.

Chapter Four

After lunch, Ellie held the merbaby and Anna tried to feed her with the bottle. Joe watched. The merbaby pushed the bottle away with her little fists and cried and cried.

"She's not going to drink it," said

Ellie, rocking her.

"Wait," said Anna. She took the lid and the teat off the bottle and dipped her finger in the milk. Then she pressed her finger against the merbaby's lips.

The merbaby licked the drop of milk and then looked with big eyes at Anna. She started to suck Anna's finger.

"She's sucking! I saw them do this with lambs on TV," said Anna.

Anna kept dripping the milk onto her finger and letting the merbaby suck it off. It was very slow. She tried again with the bottle but the merbaby wouldn't take it.

"At least she's had something," said Anna.

Then Ellie rocked her and Anna and Joe sang 'Rock-a-bye baby'. The merbaby soon closed her eyes.

"Where should she sleep?" asked Anna.

"I think she needs to sleep underwater like in the sea," said Ellie. "Put her in the bucket."

"That water smells," said Joe, bending over it. "I think she's done a wee in it."

"I'll fill it with fresh water from the bath tap," said Anna.

The merbaby blinked as Ellie lowered her into the bucket of clean water. She went right under and closed her eyes.

Anna didn't sleep well that night. She kept checking if the merbaby was still asleep.

Then, in the morning, they had a shock. The merbaby had a red rash on her face and body. Her tail was not shiny or flapping.

"She looks ill," said Ellie. "Maybe it was the milk. She might be allergic to cow's milk like my friend Tilly."

"She needs to eat something," said Anna. "What can we feed her, Ellie?"

"Let's look in the cupboard," said Ellie.

They found a tin of sardines and Ellie
struggled to open it. The merbaby did
lick a little of it from Anna's finger but
the rash didn't go. She looked very poorly.
   "What are we going to do?"
asked Anna.

Chapter Five

"Maybe it's the water!" said Ellie. "Tap water isn't salty like seawater. Maybe that's made her skin go funny."

"We could put some salt in it," said Anna.

"We won't know how much," said Ellie. "I think we should fetch some water from the sea."

They asked Mum if they could go for a walk to the sea. Mum said she would come with them.

"I'm going to see if I can carry a full bucket of seawater all the way back to the cottage without spilling any," said Anna.

"Are you sure?" said Mum.

Anna nodded.

Back at the cottage, they put the merbaby into the seawater. She looked happier. By the evening the red rash had gone. They sang nursery rhymes to her and she smiled.

The next morning, the merbaby looked poorly again.

"What is it now?" asked Anna. "What shall we do?"

"I don't think we can look after her," said Ellie. "We don't know how. We should put her back in the sea."

"But she'll be eaten by a big fish or a shark!" cried Anna. "She needs looking after. Can't we take her to a doctor or a vet?"

"Don't be silly," said Ellie. "They'll take her away – put her on show like in a zoo."

"She knows us now," said Anna. "She likes us. If only we could get her to eat more."

"Well I'm going downstairs," said Ellie. "You can do what you like."

Anna tried. She mashed some sardines with a little milk and put it on her finger. After a while the merbaby licked a little sardine and then a little more.

Anna could hear Ellie coming up the stairs.

"She's eating!" Anna called.

But it wasn't Ellie. It was Mum.

"Who's eating?" Mum asked.

Anna held the merbaby close like a

29

baby, wrapping her towel over her.

"My doll," said Anna. "She was poorly and now she's feeling better."

"That's good," said Mum, smiling.

The merbaby was wriggling. Anna tried to hold her still. Luckily Mum didn't see.

"Where's Joe?" asked Anna.

"He's made a little friend," said Mum. "The family on holiday next door have a boy his age called Lewis. They're playing outside."

Mum went downstairs.

The merbaby gurgled. Anna held her up and her tail flapped as she laughed. She was so sweet. Anna loved her so much.

"I'll look after you always," Anna told her. "You don't have to worry."

But the next morning, they did have to worry.

"Anna!" It was Ellie calling. "Look!"

A big car had pulled up outside the cottage. Two men were climbing out. One held a TV camera. The men were walking up to the cottage door. They must have found out about the merbaby.

Chapter Six

"How do they know? Who told them?" asked Anna.

"Come on," said Ellie. "We've got to get her out of here."

As fast as fish, Anna and Ellie were down the stairs and out of the back door of the cottage. Anna held the merbaby in her arms.

"Where are we going?" Anna whispered, following Ellie through the gate at the bottom of the garden. Anna looked back towards the cottage. The back door was opening. Mum and the two men were coming out.

"Come on! They've seen us!" said Ellie.

33

The two girls ran faster and faster, towards the sea and towards the place where they had found the merbaby.

Ellie crawled down behind a rock and pulled Anna down beside her. Anna opened her arms and looked at the merbaby, who stared back with scared eyes.

"We have to put her back," said Ellie, "back in the sea. There's nothing else for it."

Anna opened her mouth to argue but then shut it again. Ellie was right. Anna felt the tears rolling down her face. She could taste them, wet and salty like the sea.

"I love you," she told the merbaby, "but we have to put you back in the sea. It's the safest place."

"Come on, quickly!" said Ellie. "Give her to me!"

But Anna held the merbaby tight and carried her towards the sea. The tide was in; it was not so far to go. She leaned over by a rock and lowered the merbaby gently into the water.

The merbaby splashed and looked up in surprise.

"Swim!" Anna told her. "Swim as far away as you can!"

But the merbaby stayed in the same place, her head out of the water, flicking her tail.

"She won't swim away! They'll catch her!" cried Anna.

The men were not far behind.

"Swim! Swim!" Anna called again.

The merbaby twirled in the water and looked at Anna. But she still didn't swim away.

At that moment a wave rose up beside the merbaby. She went under the water and then surfaced again. Anna glimpsed a big fish tail.

"It's a fish!" she cried. "It's a big fish

and it's going to eat her! Oh, Ellie!"

Then Anna gasped. It wasn't a fish. Rising from the water was a beautiful woman with green eyes and long flowing curls. Her big fish tail shimmered under the water.

"A mermaid!" said Ellie.

The merbaby looked at the mermaid and laughed. The mermaid reached out her arms.

"It's her mum!" Anna whispered in amazement.

The mermaid scooped the merbaby up. The merbaby clung to her, happily.

The mermaid turned to Anna and Ellie. She gave them a smile and a wave as if to say thank you. The children waved back and watched as the mermaid and merbaby slipped away under the water.

Chapter Seven

As Anna and Ellie stared at the rippling sea, there was a panting sound behind them. Anna turned. The men had reached them and Mum followed, carrying Joe.

"I'm sorry, I'm sorry," sobbed Joe. "I only told Lewis and he promised to

keep it a secret but he told his dad.
He's not my friend anymore. Where's
the merbaby?"

"Yes," said the smaller man, in a gruff
voice. "Where's this merbaby?"

Anna couldn't speak. She met
Ellie's eyes.

"What merbaby?" asked Ellie. "What
on earth is a merbaby? What are you
talking about?"

"A baby mermaid," said the man. "We
understand you found her."

"Because Joe said so?" laughed Ellie.
"Do you always believe what four-year-
olds tell you? Joe has a very good
imagination, you know."

Anna was impressed with how
confident Ellie sounded.

"If there's no merbaby, then what were

you carrying and why were you running off?" the larger man asked.

Anna gulped. What was Ellie going to say now?

"It was a seal pup," said Ellie. "We caught it and we were looking after it. It wasn't well so we put it back in the sea. Do you really believe in mermaids – a big grown-up man like you?"

The man's face went redder.

"I did try to tell you," said Mum.

"It would have been the news story of the summer," the man grumbled.

"Well, there is no merbaby and no story," said Mum. "I think you'd better go."

The two men turned and began to walk away.

"What nasty men," said Mum. "But

you really should have told me about
the seal pup."

Mum began to walk back with Joe.
Anna looked out to sea. The waves
tumbled gently but there was nothing
else to be seen. The mermaid and her
baby would be far away by now.

"I miss her, but I'm glad she's with her
mum," Anna whispered to Ellie.

Ellie nodded and smiled. She took
Anna's hand and they walked back
towards the house.

If you enjoyed this story, why not read another *Skylarks* book?

Josie's Garden
by David Orme and Martin Remphry

Josie lives in a high-rise flat in town with her mum and brother. More than anything else in the world, Josie wants a garden. When Josie and her friend, Meena, discover an abandoned and overgrown garden near their school, Josie is delighted and decides to make the garden her own. But sometimes, things are not quite as simple as they first seem…

Carving the Sea Path

by Kathryn White and Evelyne Duverne

When Samuel first moves to the Arctic, he is rude and unfriendly. But Irniq gives him a chance, and the boys become friends. Then, as the summer comes to an end, the boys quarrel and drift apart again. One day, Irniq finds a trapped whale under the ice, and doesn't know what to do. Luckily, Samuel appears and knows exactly who can help. Will the boys save the whale in time?

The Lion and the Gypsy
by Jillian Powell and Heather Deen

Fatima the wandering gypsy is tired and lies down to sleep. A sand-coloured lion roams through the desert. He is hungry and looking for tasty morsels to eat. He stops and sniffs the air, and the scent of a human reaches his nose. He follows the footprints and, on silent paws, he creeps around the sleeping gypsy, sniffing hungrily. Fatima has no idea of the danger she is in…

The Emperor's New Clothes
by Louise John and Serena Curmi

There once lived an emperor who was proud and vain and spent all his money on clothes. One day, two scoundrels arrived at the palace and persuaded the emperor that they could weave magical cloth. He set them to work making him the finest robes he would ever own. But the emperor had a lesson to learn, and his new clothes were quite a sight to behold!